KU-015-918
USA AIRLINES
NAME Miss Polly Price
ADDRESS 3 Laurel Walk, London, England, ~~Europ~~ European Union
DESTINATION San Francisco, USA
PHONE NUMBER 01702 431689
Right now, I'm not sure if...
I ♥ SF
London Theatre Weekly
'TORN ASUNDER' to tour USA

and useful

IMPORTANT ITEMS

I MUST REMEMBER TO PACK

Pyjama trousers

BATTERYIES for my MP3

Make up remover (for Mum)

Nail Polish remover (for Mum)

Corn Plasters (for Mum)

Earplugs (just incase my MP3 player stops working)

I forgot these last time - it was VERY ~~humiliatyating~~ ~~embarass~~ annoying

TORN ASUNDER SET TO ROCK WEST COAST OF AMERICA

Arabella Diamonte is the unexpected choice to lead the cast in this World War Two drama revival. The play opened in London to mixed reviews, but the inspired casting of Daniel Hopkins as the Head of Gestapo, Otto Schmidt, promises an entertaining evening.

Important Fact about The American Flag
It has 50 stars
and 13 stripes (I counted)

INVERCLYDE LIBRARIES
GOUROCK LIBRARY

16 MAY 2019	13 AUG 2019	
29 AUG 2019		
	27 MAR 2020	
- 4 AUG 2022	24 SEP 2022	2 OCT 2022
- 3 NOV 2022	18 APR 2023	31 AUG 2023
	24 FEB 2024	

This book is to be returned on or before the last date above. It may be borrowed for a further period if not in demand.

For enquiries and renewals Tel: (01475) 712323
www.inverclyde.gov.uk/libraries

Library
Inverclyde Libraries

WITHDRAWN

Inverclyde Libraries
3 41 0600354001 5

ME
leaning out of a taxi window taking this photo with my phone.

FLASH

Diagram of the food (?) on the plane.

orange juice. They'd run out of coke

chocolate mint good

tea bad

chocolate ~~moose~~ mousse. Good.

slimy cheese

~~Wierd~~ weird salad with (yuk) olives

water good for washing down slimy meal

Possibly potatoes?

~~Merky~~ murky brown slime

supposed to be chicken – I don't think so!

biscuit to eat with slimy cheese

CHECKLIST of things to do before travelling

1) Hide Mum's green shoes

2) PACK

3a) Try to ~~cashully~~ casually say goodbye to Keira at school in front of Robbie Kildaire.

3b) Try to find a way to mention my trip to Robbie as this might impress him - as long as he doesn't learn WHY we are going.

5) Buy NOTEBOOK

It is really hard to fit 13 stripes in to a flag. It is even harder to fit 50 stars onto such a TINY blue square. I only managed 21

THINGS I'VE FOUND OUT ABOUT SAN FRANCISCO

1) It has a Golden Bridge (but it doesn't exactly look golden to me - more orange

2) It has a BEACH!!! Yay!

3) A Zoo!

4) An aquarium

5) It doesn't have the Statue of Liberty

6) It doesn't have Hollywood

This is officially the colour I would call GOLDEN

MY TOTALLY SECRET DIARY: ON STAGE IN AMERICA
A RED FOX BOOK 978 1 862 30423 9

First published in Great Britain by Doubleday,
an imprint of Random House Children's Books
A Random House Group Company

Doubleday edition published 2008
Red Fox edition published 2012

3 5 7 9 10 8 6 4 2

Text and illustrations copyright © Dee Shulman, 2008

The right of Dee Shulman to be identified as the author and illustrator of this work has been asserted in accordance with the Copyright, Designs and Patents Act 1988.

All rights reserved. No part of this publication may be reproduced, stored in a retrieval system, or transmitted in any form or by any means, electronic, mechanical, photocopying, recording or otherwise, without the prior permission of the publishers.

The Random House Group Limited supports the Forest Stewardship Council® (FSC®), the leading international forest certification organization. Our books carrying the FSC label are printed on FSC®-certified paper. FSC is the only forest certification scheme endorsed by the leading environmental organizations, including Greenpeace. Our paper procurement policy can be found at www.**randomhouse**.co.uk/environment.

Text handwritten by Dee Shulman

Red Fox Books are published by Random House Children's Books,
61–63 Uxbridge Road, London W5 5SA

www.**kids**at**randomhouse**.co.uk
www.**totallyrandombooks**.co.uk
www.**randomhouse**.co.uk

Addresses for companies within The Random House Group Limited can be found at:
www.**randomhouse**.co.uk/offices.htm

THE RANDOM HOUSE GROUP Limited Reg. No. 954009

A CIP catalogue record for this book is available from the British Library.

Printed and bound in Singapore

My Totally Secret Diary

On Stage in America

(with mostly awful actorish people, ~~espesh~~ especially the girls)

Belonging entirely to me,

Polly Price

So PLEASE KEEP OUT!

RENFREWSHIRE LIBRARIES

Dee Shulman

July 24th

Some kids have happy, carefree lives...

with NORMAL parents...
eating NORMAL food...

saying NORMAL things...

Did you have a nice day at school, dear?

Sadly I am not one of them. I am the **tragic** victim of a HOPELESS parent.

And I can think of only one way to deal with my misery, and that's to write it all down.

So this is my

DIARY OF GLOOM

This was never meant to be my diary of gloom. It's not even a real diary. It's actually the SPECIAL OFFER notebook I bought yesterday with my holiday money.

I wasn't even going to start using it till I got to America and had some stuff to stick in it - like my plane ticket, postcards, maps and other important documents of my journey.

SPACE RESERVED FOR IMPORTANT JOURNEY DOCUMENT No 1

This was the only thing that sitted - TRULY DISGUSTING! ~~Cinomon~~ cinnamon gum - the WORST invention EVER

In actual fact this book was lying happily at the bottom of my suitcase, with a few other specially chosen items...

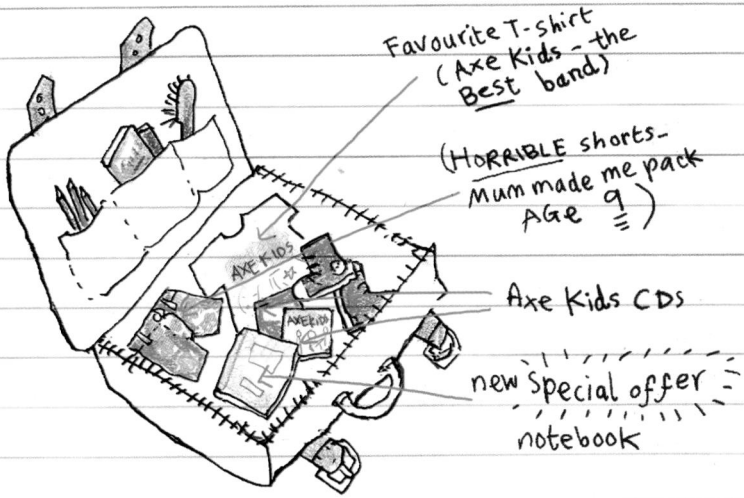

...But desperation forced me to ~~misapropriate~~ take it out and use it.

When I say desperation I am not exaggerating.

I had been packed and ready for DAYS.

Mum, on the other hand, hadn't.

The HOPELESS parent

Mum started packing when the taxi driver arrived.

By the time he was onto his 3rd cup of herbal tea -

I HAD to take action.

I just can't decide what to pack, Polly-dolly! Should I take the **PINK**? Does the colour really suit me? I **love** the **blue** linen but it creases **so** badly... and the **black**, which is so versatile, might look a bit... well - **black** - in America...

In the end we compromised. She took <u>everything</u>.

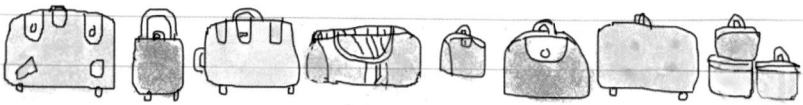

And me and the taxi driver lugged it into the taxi.

I am now sitting in that very taxi, taking deep calming ~~breths~~ breaths and trying to keep my pen from tearing through the page of my lovely new notebook. Mum is sitting cross-legged next to the taxi driver, chanting =

Doringa-gaw-gaw-Nicker-anga.....

BLACK-CAB **RECEIPT**

AMOUNT £ 7.50

Don't bother looking those words up. Mum invented them. She is repeating them in a slow *droning* voice. They are supposed to keep her **centred**. They aren't ~~keeping~~ <u>me</u> ~~centered~~ centred though. <u>PLUS</u> the chanting is making it very difficult to ~~consent~~ concentrate on writing.

So I'm going to draw some pictures till she finally gets centred.

shuts up

ME

NAME Polly – not a cool name, especially when your mother adapts it to Pollypop (or worse). But I will never reveal what Polly is short for

AGE Nearly 12

JOB Trying to keep SANE

MUM

NAME Arabella Diamonte (I think she made it up herself)

AGE Thirty-something

JOB Actress
(need I say more?)

At last! She's stopped chanting and is reapplying her make-up. This should give me loads of time to fill in some ~~relevant~~ ~~rett~~ relevant facts... like:

WHERE WE ARE GOING Answer: San Francisco!

WHY Answer: The play my mum's in...

TORN ASUNDER

...is opening there, and I'm going too – if we ever make it onto the plane.

Looking at me now you'd never guess that I've been looking forward to this FOR WEEKS.

Hey - We've arrived at the airport!!!

Gotta go!

ON THE PLANE

Because we were so late, Mum managed to persuade the staff all her luggage was

ESSENTIAL! My shoes are vital! HATS - absolutely imperative -

Ok, ok, get them on the plane!

We'd just squeezed past all the **PUNCTUAL** people into the last 2 seats... when Mum stood up.

I can't possibly sit in THIS SEAT! There's no room for my LEGS! I will only be comfortable in an AISLE seat!

The stewardess's smile had started to look distinctly like a snarl!

WOULD YOU KINDLY SIT DOWN, MADAM - WE ARE ABOUT TO TAKE OFF!

Mum refused to sit down. LOUDLY.

Everyone shuffled uncomfortably. Especially the long-legged man in the aisle seat next to me.

I knew she'd win.
It was just a matter of time.

23 seconds to be precise.

We exchanged looks of resigned misery.

Mum, on the other hand, was all happiness and joy.

Isn't this exciting, Pollypops? I just **LOVE** travelling by air!

Happiness and joy at Mum's level must be tiring, because as soon as we took off she fell asleep.

Mum must **NEVER** see this (taken with my mobile)

This has given me the perfect peace and quiet to catch up on the whole journey so far.

I think I've even got time to add some impressive ~~geo~~ ~~geogra~~ geography information.

According to the little TV screen in front of me—

Not even a bit blurry!

Uh-Oh! Mum's just stood up. BAD SIGN.

Aghh!
She's waving!
DANIEL, DARLING! Is the whole cast on the plane? How marvellous!
She's clambering over passengers - I can't look!
WAIT— the head steward has stepped in...
MADAM - this is not - - My GOODNESS... You're not A-A-Arabella-?
I am She!
regal voice
H-H-How utterly thrilling! Is there anything I can do for you?
BAD MOVE - stew-boy
dazzling smile
Why, you SWEET man - there is one TINY thing you could do...

The company and I would so LOVE to have a little party - perhaps in the First Class section - to cause less of a disturbance?

Mum looking around ~~compash~~ ~~compasson~~ compassionately

Well - ahem - absolutely! It's quite empty in there actually.

flattened

He's rewarded by one of Mum's suffocating hugs. But he seems truly happy, leading Mum and all the actors away.

I slide down in my seat. If I shut my eyes they may go without me...

BUM.

not quite sure

LATER (that day/night)

USEFUL TIP

If you close your eyes for long enough and turn your MP3 player up really loud you can actually block out your mother and her friends and even fall asleep.

But it takes a lot of hard ~~consen~~ concentration and it is NOT pleasant to be woken up again.

I looked at my watch ... nearly MIDNIGHT!

I looked out the window... Sunshine?

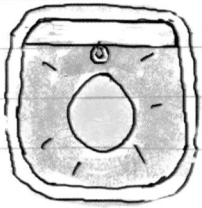

never will my true name be revealed

Really [redacted], Polly! Has that dreadful Miss Pukeit taught you nothing about international time differences? What does she do all day?

Actually – Miss Pugitt

Now please stop blinking inanely at your watch - I'd like to get to the hotel before the first performance.

YET ANOTHER RELEVANT DOCUMENT OF JOURNEY

Can't remember much about the journey from the airport - I must have dozed off again. But I am now in a

SAN FRANCISCO HOTEL

sitting - well, lying, on a big comfy bed

July 25th Next Morning (or so they say)

Breakfast, Polly-poppet - come along!

She's just woken me up AGAIN.

The truth is I've been dragged around by my mum long enough not to let details like waking up in a strange bed worry me.

I HAVE STRATEGIES

On this occasion I decided the best strategy was to shut my eyes and go back to sleep.

I've just woken up again — STARVING... and my brain is now working well enough to fix on one important word - Breakfast

To find breakfast requires me to activate

EMERGENCY STRATEGY NO. 2 - The Nose (This has never failed me)

THE NOSE in this case meant following the divine hotel breakfast smell ... down 2 flights of stairs into – YES...

THE DINING ROOM!!!

Mum would have been hard to miss.

I sat down opposite her.

I thought Americans spoke English!

The best I could do in the ~~ee~~ circumstances was point at the plate Mum was tucking into, which was filled with...

Mum's eating **MEAT**??? She's supposed to be **VEGETARIAN!**
Actually she's supposed to be **VEGAN** ← the PUREST kind of vegetarian
At least she has been for the past 8 months - since she entered her ~~BUDDIS~~ ~~BUDH~~ BUDDHIST Phase ←

So I'm sitting here watching Mum stuffing sausages and **fried eggs** into her mouth...

also NOT Allowed! ↗

... and I am **UTTERLY SPEECHLESS** →

PLONK!

WOW!
LOOK what's just landed in front of me! →

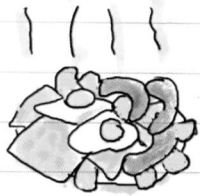

MUM'S BUDDHIST PHASE - Total Nighmare! Mum turning Vegan has meant **ME** giving up everything I love: Sweets chocolate, custard, ice cream, sausages, nuggets, treacle pudding etc. Mum wouldn't even let me eat chips (which I've recently found out Vegans are allowed) because she believes ALL FRIED FOOD is POISON. So practically all we've been allowed to eat for MONTHS is beans and rice. And salad. I'm Probably clinically ~~malnurish~~ starved.

I have just decided that UTTERLY SPEECHLESS outrage is important - but not as important as scoffing the lot before Mum turns Vegan again.

Uh-oh - She has just stood up.

But the show's been on in London for a year - you must know it by now!

Raised eyebrow and withering look →

I give up! Good job this diary's secret.

Hyppolita - how many years have you been associated with me?

Is this how a normal mother talks?

Surely even a child of your limited observational skills will have noticed by now that every theatre is different? The staging has to be adapted. After all - we have to put on a glorious show for our American audience...

radiant smile for possible American audience in room →

And of course the **children** are still quite new to the play...

What children?

Heavens above, child, does your brain retain nothing? The-children-in-the-cast! This will be a marvellous opportunity for you to meet them.

Before I can come up with an ESCAPE strategy, I am being dragged out of the hotel and along the streets of San Francisco. It's not at all easy to catch up with your diary every time you stop at a crossing.

Especially if you have a mother who keeps jogging you when she grabs your shoulder to cross the road

IMPORTANT JOURNEY DOCUMENT
spotted on ground by traffic light!

THE THEATRE - A bit later

Things are not good.

My mum has just WOOSHED us through a bunch of actors, towards 2 whispering girls...

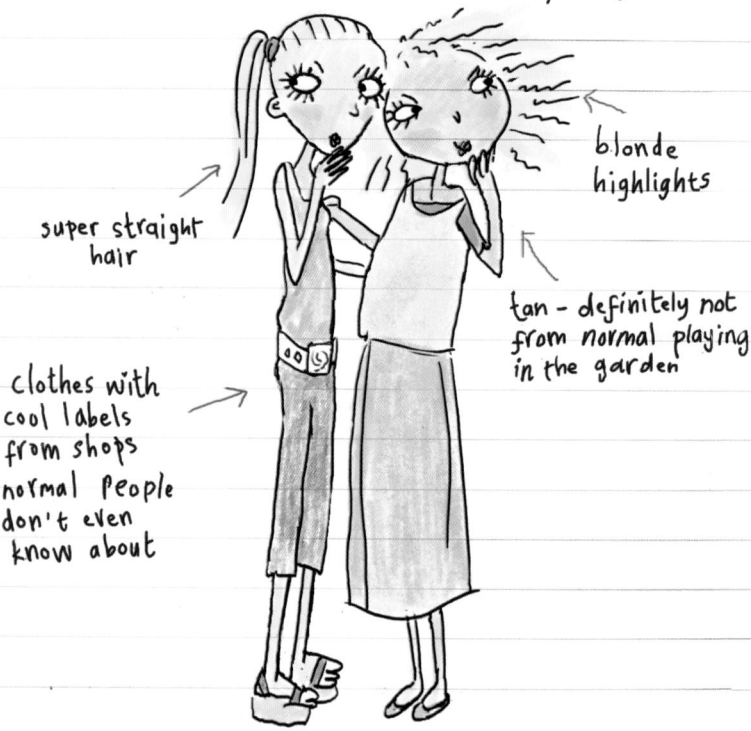

... girls who were instantly ~~recon~~ recognizable as CHILD ACTORS.

* IMPORTANT NOTE *

THEATRE KIDS

Most kids hanging around theatres are there because they have no choice. They are the tragic victims of show-off parents, who drag them around the place, forcing them to read old comics in total silence, for hours in pokey dressing rooms.

I am obviously in this catergory

But then there's this other breed of kid:

THE CHILD ACTOR

He or she is there because she wants to be there. You can usually rely on the fact that THE CHILD ACTOR is the last child on earth who any normal person (me) would want to spend their summer in San Francisco hanging round with.

Back to the whispering girls...

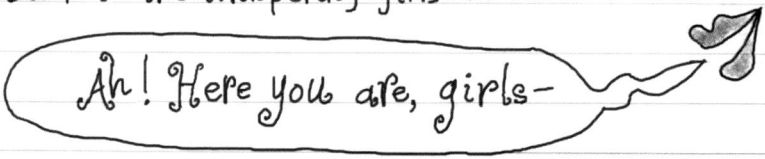

The two blonde highlights looked absolutely thrilled at having their conversation interrupted.

~~Mirak~~ Miraculously - I am saved from further torture by the perfectly-timed arrival of...

... NIGEL - the Director

The actors are all spellbound, so I've managed to sneak away from the girls and found a ~~secluo~~ secluded seat. From here I can check everyone out. Most eyes are gazing adoringly at Nigel, but I've just caught 2 ⊙ ⊙ staring straight back at me! Below the eyes ◡ is a mouth, which is grinning.

It belongs to a face I haven't seen before - a boy, a couple of years older than me probably. But he looks way too normal (nice) to be one of the **actor kids**. So whose poor son can he be? I can't see anyone who looks much like him — WAIT - there's another boy, also blond, about the same age!

THIS PLACE IS LITTERED WITH KIDS!

Blah blah – darlings... drone blah drone

The second boy hasn't spotted me – he's totally ~~fokus~~ ~~focusse~~ concentrating on Ophelia and Aurora... They've just passed him a note.

Now all 3 are collapsing with laughter.

SNORT

LUCKILY FOR THEM nobody has noticed because Nigel has just run out of drone so everyone is breaking for coffee – ~~exe~~ except the stage managers, who are getting stuff ready for the ~~reher~~ rehearsal.

Actually I'm quite looking forward to this rehearsal now – ok – I actually can't wait to see the BLONDE HIGHLIGHTS trying to act like REAL people!

OH NO!

Something red and dangerous is coming over –

Darling – the children aren't needed today – so our TREASURE of a ~~sha~~ chaperone, Donna, has agreed that after lessons, she will take you along with the other children into San Francisco! Aren't you lucky?

Would you describe being stuck all afternoon with Ophelia, Aurora and Donna as **lucky**?

I don't think so.

Er - actually, Mum - I was looking forward to watching you rehearse.

This **had** to work...

How touching, darling! But tomorrow's rehearsal will be much better to watch - and this trip will be such fun! Anyway, imagine how delighted Miss Puteit will be with the extra work!

WHAT? You can't mean I have to do lessons as well?

All the children are, Polly-doodle. You don't want to fall behind now, do you?

But it's the **Summer holiday!**

I'm whining into the air. She's gone.

LATER

Before I had a chance to call the American Child Abuse Agency, Donna hauled me into the sort of pokey room that theatres specialize in...

THE THEATRE GREEN ROOM

Don't ask me why it's called a green room. I've never seen one that was actually green.

Aurora took this photo with her instant camera- and THREW it away!! (I fished it out- recognizing an important document)

no window

Dank paper cup with remains of coffee in it. This one also has ~~floors~~ bright red lipstick decorating the rim.

smell of stale cigarettes in spite of NO SMOKING sign

Apart from these unsavoury items, the room also contained Aurora and Ophelia... along with the 2 boys I'd spotted in the auditorium.

Donna chose herself the least stained chair, folded herself into it, and picked up a magazine.

Aurora and Ophelia groaned.

The boy who'd been passing notes sat down by the girls and got a book out. He didn't open it though. He just whispered something to them, and they all started vibrating with laughter.

The other boy cleared his throat.

Hi, I'm Will.

He's way better looking than this (I've rubbed this drawing out about 20 times)

I liked him.
What was he doing here?

And that's Felix – we're sharing the role of Hugo in the play. Have you met the girls?

I was just about to answer, but Ophelia got there first.

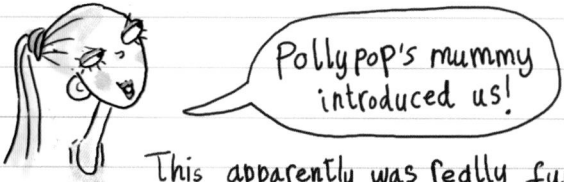

This apparently was really funny.

Will ignored them.

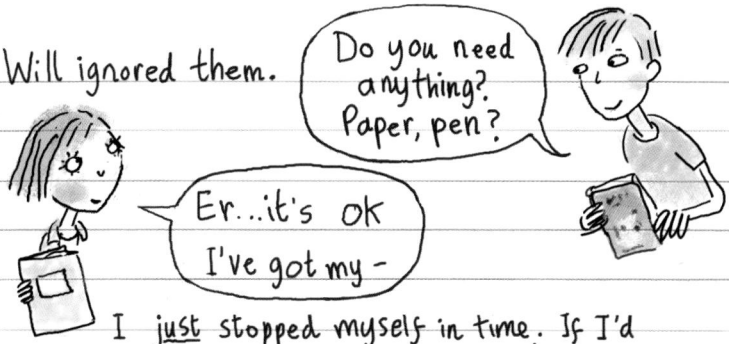

I just stopped myself in time. If I'd said DIARY in here, I'd be **dead**.

We sat down at a ropey old table. He got out a couple of books and started to read. I opened my diary really carefully so no one could see inside, and I've managed to catch up on today's events ~~extree~~ extremely ~~efish~~ efficiently.

Will Will William will Will Will WILL

I like the name **WILL**. I hope it's short for William William William

BUM! What was I thinking??? Now I have to buy some white correction stuff IMMEDIATELY.

Hey - looks like we're on the move. Donna has just put down her magazine and stood up.

LATER

We all trooped out into brilliant sunshine.

Will gave me an ~~exhasp~~ exasperated look, and I tried not to laugh.

PHEW! Comic strips take totally AGES to do!

Luckily for those of us who don't like stupid arguments (ME), Ron arrived, and put his arm round Donna, causing Ophelia and Aurora to:

(1) Shut up
(a very good result)

... then

(2) whisper
(not so good but still less annoying than arguing.)

Blissfully unaware, Ron and Donna set off towards the Shopping mall with the rest of us trailing behind.

The mall was MASSIVE!!!

I would have taken a million photos if I hadn't left my mobile back at the hotel. Anyway I was so busy staring that it took me a while to notice Aurora's growing whine...

I'M STARVINGGG!

Huh! Starving but totally picky...

Euch! I'm not eating there!

-or there!

-or there!

Eventually EVERYONE was starving.

The diner that passed the Princess Aurora test was on the 5th floor (nothing suitable on floors 1–4). But I have to admit this one was utterly DAZZLING!

I hoisted myself happily up onto this stool.

Donna pulled me off it.

We're sitting at the tables.

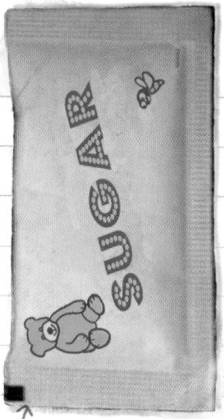

cute bear!
YET ANOTHER IMPORTANT JOURNEY DOCUMENT

Donna and Ron sat opposite each other kissing a lot.

Ophelia and Aurora sat next to each other giggling a lot.

Felix and Will sat by me, eating a lot

– and they'd just started telling some really good jokes... when the bill came. Donna examined it, then told us that we each owed $9.

OK – I never wrote about the moment when my mum gave me a ~~wad~~ wad of money, and said, 'Have a great time, darling.'

I never wrote about it for a very good reason. It didn't happen.

I had no money at all.

I wiggled my fingers around my jeans pockets anyway, hoping for a miracle, while everyone else passed bundles of dollars across to Donna.

Surely there was enough?

It looked like loads.

She counted the money.

Then she re-counted it.

For some reason, all eyes turned to me.

HA! HA! HA! HA! HA! HA!

Obviously everyone found this hilarious...

well nearly everyone.

It's OK, I've got enough to pay for Polly's. Come on, let's get out of here.

♥Will♥

I'll pay you back... ← croaked whisper

Hey, you can get mine next time.

my hero

Aurora and Ophelia were in **Princess Heaven!**

WAX
GAME EMPO
Wow! Look at the size of that Games Shop! You coming, Will?
And so we went our separate ways.

...shoes...
Ooh No, Aurora - they make your ankles look fat!

...even jewellery...
I do so love diamonds. Hey - Aurora... look! Orlando's! Party Dresses!

In Orlando's nearly everything sparkled- including the 2 assistants- whose lip gloss shimmered into action whenever Ophelia or Aurora picked anything up.
Oh my! I just know that's going to look fabulous on you! Are you looking for a special occasion?
We're going to need something really spectacular for our Opening Night.
Totally glamer glamour divine.
Are you in the show too, honey?
Eyelash extensions suddenly widened in my direction
Er-no...
Uhuh. So what are you then?
Who asks questions like this? No prizes for guessing who answers though...
She's nothing - just here with her mummy - SNORT!

The lashes turned quickly back to the stars.

You girls have to try these on in our Regency ~~Sweet~~ Suite - it's Zelda Rose's favourite dressing room!

Have you got anything to try on, Missy?

lip gloss suddenly beamed towards me

Er - no, it's OK.

Ha! You don't have to pay to try things on, you know, Polly-poop!

SNIGGER

Oh - get lost!

muttered not quite under my breath

Aurora snorted, and flounced off with Ophelia to the changing room, leaving me free to explore. And I have to admit the clothes were AMAZING. So amazing, that it was only when I noticed the assistants closing the doors that I looked at my watch...

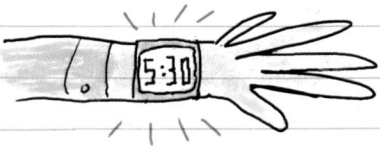

dropped off one of the dresses Ophelia took to try on

Oh no! We were supposed to meet back at the diner ½ an hour ago! I dashed to the changing rooms –

Ophelia, Aurora – we're late!

B-b-but they can't have done. We were together.

...and I was just contemplating PANIC...

...when I smelt the familiar whiff of

REGENCY SU
Sorry honey - the changing rooms are empty — your friends left about... ... half an hour ago!
I ran wildly towards the escalators, trying to work out which floor I was on, and which floor the diner was on. Neither answer came into my head.
DINER
Hooray!
burger and fries.....
this joy was to be very short-lived.
Sorry Miss - We're closed!

It took no time at all to come to a full assessment of the situation...

I leaned against the diner window and shut my eyes, which you'd think would prevent tears from getting out, but they somehow found gaps and squished their way through. My only ~~consel~~ consolation was there was no one there to notice...

CORRECTION...

By the time we got back to the theatre it was getting late - but then I heard that familiar voice echoing round the auditorium -

YOU DID WHAT?

Phew! They were still rehearsing - I hadn't been missed - BIG Relief as my mum has a slight tendency to get hysteric -

ARE YOU TELLING ME THAT YOU LEFT MY CHILD ALONE - IN THE MIDDLE OF THIS CRIME-INFESTED CITY? gasp - SOMEONE TELL ME I DIDN'T ENTRUST MY DAUGHTER'S LIFE TO THIS MORONIC LITTLE HALF-WIT! HAS ANYONE CALLED THE POLICE, THE ARMY, THE FIRE BRIGADE?

One look at Will's horrified expression confirmed my deepest fear... These weren't lines from the script.

Come on then, Poll, We'd better put her out of her misery.

THIS IS THE SCENE WE FACED
actor trying to escape while appearing to be in helpful pursuit of missing child
FIND MY CHILD
Nigel trying to work out how to use a mobile phone
Donna trying to look deeply ashamed
scurrying stage-hand (well... foot!)
It's OK, everyone – Polly's back – safe and sound.

Of course that couldn't be the end of it, could it?

After the ~~compulser~~ compulsory ~~sufer~~ suffocating sobby, soaking hug, there had to be this

MASSIVE ~~INCW~~ INQUISITION.

Mum wasn't interested in the FACTUAL version of events (mine or Will's).

She wanted BLOOD ← DONNA'S

Arabella, darling - we can't simply get rid of someone. There are all sorts of issues... and to be fair, legally - Donna's - ahem - responsibilities begin and end with the - er - child performers.
Bad tactical decision, Nigel...
Are you telling me that MY child's life is worth less than those precoshuss little princesses in the cast?
must look up this spelling
N-no - of course not, my love.
Indeed - I now wonder if perhaps I too am worth less than they are? Perhaps you will find the show a whole lot easier legally to manage without Arabella Diamonte in the starring role? (heartrending) SOB!

Arabella-darling...
big actory hug
You know the show utterly depends on your marvellous ~~paw~~ portrayal...
look of adulation
I just think we are all a bit tired and overwrought...
soothing but firm
And we should discuss this again after a good night's sleep.
My mother was not soothed.
Come on, Hyppolita. We're leaving!

Forgot to bring diary down - so got this from reception!!!

Palace Park Hotel
532 Posh St. San Francisco CA 9310 Tel. 533.1303

July 26th The Next Morning

... and No I don't feel any better.

Hunger has driven me down for breakfast, and I've been ~~lerk~~ lurking by the door, checking who's in there.

THE GOOD NEWS No sign of the girls - or Donna.

THE BAD NEWS Mum's in there... with Nigel.

So I'm going to have to skulk around out here till she - BUM - she's waving...

Hyppolita, darling - over here! You simply must try the pancakes - they're miraculous!

They must be to have caused this transformation.

oops- maple syrup!
Then my plateful of pancakes arrives...
4 pancakes! swimming in maple syrup
blueberries
~~wip~~ whipped cream
strawberries
And I begin to understand. In fact the pancakes almost completely distract me from the conversation.
Almost.
No - You're so right, Nigel, Sweetie. Poor Little Donna absolutely has to stay. I wouldn't hear of anything else!
???!!!
I MUST have misheard.

I see now that Polly was absolutely fine - probably wandered off in a world of her own. What a ~~garstly~~ ~~ghars~~ ghastly shock for
Poor Sweet Donna!
Do you know what, Nigel? I'm going to send Donna some flowers. Lilies would be perfect...
My mother is clearly having some sort of breakdown! Better take action.
Mum, can you hear me? Shall-I-call-a-doctor?

utterly blank

You know, darling – the incredibly famous and powerful Letitia Milton!
?! ? ! ?
even more utterly blank
Honestly, Hyppolita - I sometimes wonder if you weren't accidentally swapped with some stupid woman's baby in the hospital...
Letitia Milton - Donna's aunt - is the Hollywood theatre critic! And she's asked for tickets to our Opening Night! Have you any idea what a review from Letitia Milton could mean?
faraway look
Anyway, I'd better get off and order those lilies. Buck up, Polly-Lolly. We'll be leaving for the theatre in ten minutes.
How am I supposed to grow up NORMAL??
Palace Park Hotel
532 Posh St. San Francisco CA 93710 Tel. 533.1303

AN HOUR LATER

I am sitting in a dark auditorium in a dark dark mood - waiting for the rehearsal to start.

Luckily I've managed to slip into my seat more or less unnoticed.

BUT HOW LONG CAN I KEEP THIS UP ???

avoiding Donna, the princesses, and my warm forgiving mother?

At Last - the curtain's opening...

ABOUT 2 HOURS LATER (12.30pm)

Wow! I've already seen Torn Asunder about a million times, and I know it ~~practikly~~ almost off-by-heart because I've spent hours testing Mum on her lines - but that was really good!!!

The weirdest thing is, I'm finding it really hard to hate Ophelia now, because on stage she was completely different... sort of lost and fragile.

OPHELIA
(as Sarah)

wig - no sign of a highlight.

horrible ragged dress

DANIEL HOPKINS
(Prison-Camp Officer)

Daniel Hopkins played a ~~grotesk~~ ~~grotesck~~ grotesque prison-camp officer - with no consideration for human life... (especially Ron's)

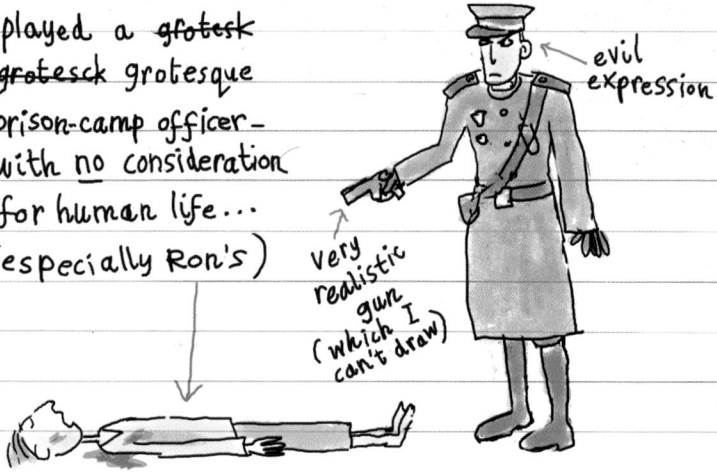

WILL
(Hugo)

Will played Ophelia's brother, who heroically managed to get them both out of the clutches of the evil Daniel Hopkins and find their mother. (guess who?)

Will was BRILLIANT!

I just have to go and congratulate ~~him~~ everyone.

A BIT LATER

I rushed up the corridor and opened the first dressing-room door. BAD MOVE.

I had to settle for a strangulated gurgle, but just about managed to turn round and walk out.

I got halfway down the corridor when I heard footsteps behind me. I was not going to turn round.
Polly - slow down!
That was not Ophelia's voice.
Will?
I take it you didn't think much of the run-through?
Er-no-Will, no! I mean-yes-I-it-was-er...
What was the matter with my mouth today? The best it could manage was-
Er..you...it-was er... great...

Fortunately Will didn't seem to notice I'd lost the power of speech.

Especially tomorrow!
What's happening tomorrow?
Just the small matter of the Opening cast list...
me - trying not to look blank (and failing)
The director's final decision about which two kids will play Sarah and Hugo for the Opening Night... the show all the Press are coming to.
Oh yes...
Oh NO !!! It'll be a...
BLOOD BATH!

You coming then, Will?
Ominous shapes at the end of the corridor
Me trying to disguise myself as a portion of corridor wall
Oh yeah - we're off to the diner across the road for a sandwich. Do you want to come?
Er - I don't think so!
Shall I bring you something back, then?
But I still owe you for the diner yesterday.
You can pay me back when you get some money - I'm on a salary don't forget, so I'm loaded. What do you like?
Everything!

Now that he's gone I have to admit there are one or two things I don't like:

Olives ← how could anyone eat these?

goat's cheese ← too smelly to put on a plate - let alone in a mouth

fishpaste yuk

fish pie yuk

fish curry yuk

fish burgers OK... anything with fish in it

coleslaw ← who came up with such a stupid idea?

bananas when they've been in your school bag for 10 minutes. →

pickled onions YUK!

Cabbage ← EUCH!

bread with bits in →

meat with lumps in →

capers ← who invented these?

Mushrooms like eating slugs →

~~avert~~ avocado pear like eating slugs →

AGGHH!!! what'll I do when Will comes back with something I can't eat?

LATER

The Good News

The brown paper bag that Will handed me...

contained an EGG ~~BAY BAGUL~~ BAGEL

not a single mushroom or pickled onion to be seen!

The Bad News

I was just sitting in heavenly happiness next to Will, biting joyfully into my egg bagel, when...

Darling — I've been looking for you EVERYWHERE! I thought I'd find you with those charming girls Azalea and Oregano.

Her mouth suddenly snapped shut as she stood staring down at us.

During the silent lull, my heart sank. I just knew she was about to say something utterly ~~hidius~~ ~~hidious~~ hideous – like...

Has Pollypops got a little crush on you, Will?

or...

Hyppolita – I forbid you to sit with boys until you are twenty-one!

What she actually said was:

POLLY! You're eating WHITE bread! After all I've taught you about the benefits of the whole grain! Warren – a whole grain means a happy bowel –

I HAD to stop her.
MUM!
Er... I - er - really enjoyed the rehearsal this morning.
desperate change of subject
Really, darling? But the lights went out during the tender love scene.
SUCCESS!
Well it looked great to me - so how good will it be when the lights are working?
Oh Polly - you ARE precious!
BIG LIPSTICKY HUG!

Are you watching this afternoon's rehearsal?
Probably. Did I have a choice?
Oh Polly-doodle - I am so pleased you're taking such an interest. Perhaps there is a Thespian deeply buried in that unexpected frame! See you later, darling — Walter, you'd better get yourself changed, we're starting at two.
I think this is Mum-speak for actory person - so obviously I pray there isn't one buried deep in my unexpected frame!
I'm only needed for a couple of scenes — do you want to come and hang out in the Green Room?
I was torn -
Should I go with Will (and maybe face the girls)?
OR
Stay here alone?
Who was I kidding?

THE GREEN ROOM

Will lent me this as I left my notebook in the auditorium

Oops! It's really thin paper

Aurora stared ominously at the discarded red taffeta on the floor...

She picked it up and held it against herself.

To be honest she looked OK - not fat at all - and I might have even told her, if she'd asked my opinion.

But she wasn't interested in what I thought.
Well, Will? How do I look? My dancing teacher says I have the grace of an angel.
She did her best to demonstrate this.
I did my best to keep a straight face.
I wish we could dance in the play. I suppose it's too tragic for dancing...
But you'd think there'd be an opportunity to sing, wouldn't you? Singing is my first love.
no idea how to spell this name
My voice teacher Giseppy Jigliany (yes the Gisseppi Jigglyani) told my mother that I could be truly sensational!
I'll sing you one of my favourites, shall I?

She didn't wait for an answer.
Darknessssss
Oh where is the moonlight?
Guide me far
From this black night
And take me awayyyy
The ~~first~~ recital went on and on, each verse more warbly than the last - so by the time she finished, my head was throbbing.
That was - er - um - extraordinary, Aurora!
Oh thank you, Will! But I think I sing the dying love song from 'Angels' even better.
I can imagine, Aurora - but maybe you should rest your voice? We're opening the day after tomorrow.

Oh - singing's good for my voice - it needs lots of exercise. I'd better run through the high notes first...
Eeeeeeoooooo—
AURORA!!!! What are you doing in my dress?
For one moment I actually felt sorry for Aurora - I needn't have.
Really, Ophelia - the red taffeta should be my dress. I tried it on first. And Will thinks I look better in it than you - don't you, Will?
Will blinking in shock.
Will, how could you? Just get that dress off right now, Aurora - or I'll never speak to you again.

Then Ophelia suddenly turned to me.

Will sped off, with me a milli-second behind him - no way was I staying in there without him. So I've spent the rest of the afternoon hiding in the auditorium, watching bits of rehearsal, and catching up on writing this whenever the lights are bright enough - which has not been <u>at all</u> easy.

Nigel has just clapped his hands and called the cast together.

Marvellous, darlings - great day's work. First thing tomorrow morning I shall put up the final cast list. Obviously this is a matter of particular excitement for our younger cast members...

Excitement? Er - understatement, Nigel!

And I know that you are all far too level-headed to feel serious disappointment...

What planet is he on?

The selection has nothing to to do with talent...

Yeah-right!

Any of the four of you would do a fabulous job!

Big ~~insinseer~~ insincere grin

Immediately after that we'll have our final dress rehearsal - followed by a BEACH PARTY! Donna, Rod and Daniel have kindly agreed to organize food and games - so all the rest of us have to do is find our cozzies and turn up!

JULY 27th Next Morning

Only an insane person would choose to be around the theatre when that cast list goes up, and I am NOT insane.

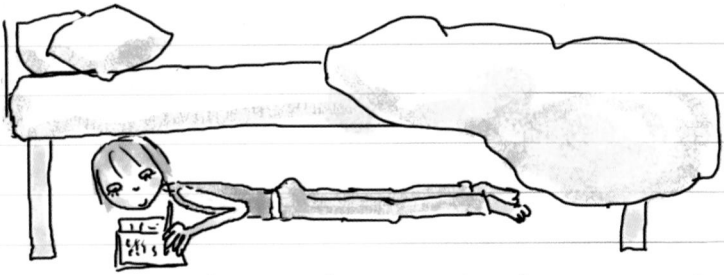

OK, hiding under the bed might not appear entirely sane - but I have to avoid detection... UH-OH!

HYPPO-DARLING?

CLOSE ONE ... but I think she's gone -

THE THEATRE - 3 seconds after arrival

Luckily the girls weren't actually killing each other - because Will and Felix were heroically preventing them.

Look! Witnesses! Everyone knows I've got a much better voice than her. She sings like a cat on heat! And my dancing teacher told—
Luckily Nigel arrived.
Donna, darling - would you be an angel, and take Aurora and Felix off to that glorious ice-cream parlour on Union Square. I want to hear you sampled the biggest and best in town...

Oh shut up, Aurora – we've all heard what your dancing teacher told your mother... it's not my fault the director ~~rekog~~ recognizes the genuine star. I don't see why you're taking it out on me... Is Felix attacking Will? No – he totally accepts that Will is the better actor for the role... And look what you've done to my arm! I'm going to phone my mother (sob) and my agent (sniff)...
Pretty masterful actually, but keeping Aurora and Ophelia apart for the whole morning has not put a lid on this situation in my opinion. I mean – if someone spread a sheet of cling-film over Mt. Vesuvius would anyone feel safe? I DON'T THINK SO! Especially if you lived in Pompeii
quite impressive proof that I listened in at least 1 history lesson.

AFTER THE REHEARSAL

ON OUR WAY TO THE BEACH PARTY

It is with no pleasure that I have to report I was right. The volcano has not been snuffed out.

I'm beginning to slightly regret ever starting on this volcano thing.

Ophelia and Aurora clapped eyes on each other as soon as we got onto the coach, and immediately started to...

And they could not be distracted.

I don't believe it – WE'RE STOPPING! The doors are opening! Got to get out before my head explodes!

USEFUL OBSERVATION

Any horrific noise coming from the mouths of ~~clinicly~~ clinically insane girls will drift painlessly away on the breeze, if you can get them off a coach and onto a beach.

It's a beautiful afternoon with a clear blue sky. Felix, Will and I have been helping Donna, Ron and Daniel lay out the rugs and food.

Got to stop writing to take some pics with my phone – Felix and Will are trying to get Seagulls to fetch sticks!

Will's given up! ↓

seagull totally ignoring Felix

THE PICNIC (on the beach)

Ophelia slumped down between me and Will.

I am totally ~~exors~~ exhausted after that rehearsal – what with all the changes... not to mention the **pressure** of carrying the role of Sarah for all the press and celebrities tomorrow night.

SHOVE

That's just ~~TIPI~~ TYPICAL of you, Ophelia - managing to show off and whine in the same sentence! You're such a —
Now then, Aurora, why don't you try some of this real American lemonade?

I WANT COKE!
Aurora! Be quiet! you're giving me a headache...
...on top of probable HEAT-STROKE...
...and - Oh NO! MOSQUITOS! I'm SO ALLERGIC!

Sweetie – if you're so worried about the noise, the heat and the mosquitos, why don't you go and sit in the coach? You could take your sandwiches.

What? In the coach? On my own? Are you joking? Unless...

For one ~~FRESH~~ PRECIOUS, GLORIOUS moment, Ophelia was lost for words.

But things weren't quiet for long...

Aurora just turned her back on everyone, and Ophelia made a dash for the sea.

Then Daniel Hopkins (who I discovered is actually not at all like a prison-camp officer) tried to perk the party up by dancing around the rugs, showering us with handfuls of...

...chocolate bars

and sweets

genuine bits of sweet wrapper

Everyone pounced on them.
I HAD to eat all these for the sake of my diary.
BLISS
Delight
CRUNCHY NUT CLUSTERS
Everyone except Aurora.
Even Ophelia (dripping with sea water instead of mayo) joined in the feast - so we all began to relax.
A BIG MISTAKE...
CHOMP
Mmm - how lovely American chocolate is! And how lucky I am that I can eat what I like and not put on an ounce...
EXPLOSION
This took the atmosphere up to → UNBEARABLE
TOTALLY EMBARRASSING
AWKWARD
TENSE
OK
Thankfully Nigel the director stepped in...
TIME FOR A GAME OF HIDE-AND-SEEK!

It was all going pretty well until it was Aurora's turn to count. She got to 100, opened her eyes, shuffled around for a couple of minutes, and then suddenly started to scream...

Just as Aurora glugged the last of the coke, Daniel burst forward –

I sat back down and have had a nearly peaceful time catching up on my diary.

apart from annoying comments from people like Ron.

Of course, in between writing and ignoring Ron, I've been keeping an eye on the treasure hunt.

Will and Aurora ↓

The 2 teams are on different sets of clues – so it's hard to tell who's winning...

...but Felix and Ophelia look a bit stuck... →

Uh-Oh! Ophelia's shouting at Daniel:

It's not **FAIR!** You purposely gave the others easier clues! And I got landed with Felix, who can't work anything out. I've had enough of this – I'm joining their team.

I don't believe it – she is actually running off to join the others...

leaving Felix SPEECHLESS!

Will and Aurora are right on the other side of the beach ... Ophelia has nearly reached them. NO... she's not running any more ... she's ...

That is the sound of her landing... followed immediately by a blood-~~cerd~~ curdling...

Everyone's running now – including me

LATER (on the coach back to the hotel)

It's been so dramatic I haven't had a chance to write anything till now! So - where was I? Oh yes - Ophelia on the sand, covered in seaweed, wailing. Nigel was first on the scene.

As Daniel and Ron carried Ophelia back up the beach, she suddenly spotted the chocolate rabbit.

And he strode over, picked it up and handed it to her.

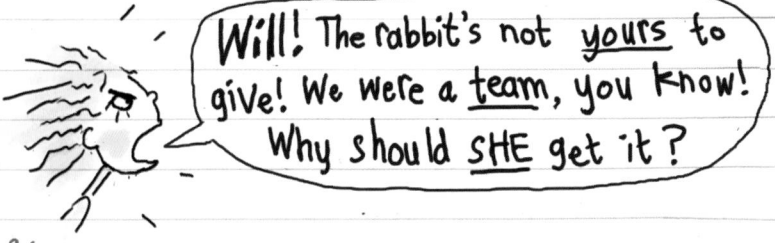

But Ophelia kept an iron grip on the rabbit all the way to the taxi...

Aurora was ~~smoled~~ smouldering by the time they'd driven off.

Nobody around here considers my feelings. It's always Ophelia, Ophelia, Ophelia. First she gets my role, then she gets MY chocolate rabbit! And I was so looking forward to it. Chocolate is very good for ~~deprech~~ depression—but nobody here would notice how deeply depressed I've been all day - because all they care about is Ophel—

Aurora!!! Why don't you just GROW UP?

Aurora's mouth snapped shut. The rest of us stared in ~~ofed~~ awed silence.

Ron broke the spell.

This went down really well...

For the first time ever Mum was NOT exaggerating. The volume was UNBEARABLE. So everyone agreed that enough was enough — it was ~~definat~~ definitely time to leave.

BACK AT THE HOTEL

As soon as we got back here - most of the company (the adults basically) vanished.

Unfortunately Aurora didn't. She stomped over to a corner of reception, and plonked herself down. Donna was with Ophelia at the hospital, so we couldn't just leave Aurora - could we?

In the end Felix got some Cokes, and we sat near her - hoping someone would finally come and release us.

At last the revolving doors revolved Nigel, Donna and Ophelia into reception. Even from where I was sitting I could see that Ophelia was not having a good face day.

Donna quickly disappeared with Ophelia into the lift, and Nigel came over to talk to us.

Well - there's nothing broken, thank the Lord! But she landed on her nose, which is, er - a little swollen... and unfortunately her ankle has got a rather nasty sprain... So she can't put any weight on it. She's getting the hang of the crutches pretty well though.

There was a moment's silence while we took this all in. Then Felix asked the question we'd all been thinking...
Will Ophelia be able to go on stage tomorrow night?
No-I'm afraid not...
Aurora, who had been sitting with her back to us, suddenly straightened.
What did you say?
It's true, Aurora-it looks like you're on for the Opening after all!
Aggh!!!! Me in front of the PRESS! And Ophelia said Joe Fitt might be there... and Amelie Rose—

I need someone to go through my lines with me, I need—
Hey - calm down, Aurora! By the sound of it, I think you need to rest your voice and get a good night's sleep. Then tomorrow—
Why are you trying to stop me practising? It's because you want me to be rubbish, isn't it? You think Ophelia's the best! Well, let me tell you, my singing teacher—
Just give it a rest, Aurora!
You're ALL against me! I HATE you, Will! You've always preferred Ophelia, and I'm just as pretty as her, and - sob - I'm a much better singer - sob - and I —

Now, now, Aurora - you don't hate anyone. You've just had some unexpected news and it's got you all jittery. What you need now is to rest your voice! The more you shout, the huskier it's getting. So I'm going to order you a nice hot drink, and you can take it up to your room.
And there's no need to worry about your lines tonight - because tomorrow I've called an extra dress rehearsal.
You see! You don't trust I'll be good enough. I bet you want me to go over that STUPID SCENE again. 'Quietly Hysterical!' You can't do—
Aurora - are you MAD? You've just been told you've got the part, and instead of being over the moon... Honestly, if it was me—
You wouldn't understand, Felix - you're just too thick-skinned to be affected by his comments—
Come along now, Aurora - this has gone on long enough. Let's go and find Donna.

July 28th - Next Morning - Way too early

Then she rudely dragged me into a sitting position, gripping my face in both her hands.

Good. So let me ask you again- how well do you know the play?
She woke me up for a quiz?
The play?
Polly- did no part of my gene pool reach your brain? The PLAY that's opening tonight!
Yes Mum - I know the play is opening tonight! I'd have to be brain-dead not to have picked up on that one.
said really slowly as if explaining a hard sum to a 6-year-old
Ok. Let me see if I can put this really simply... The - play - that - is - opening - tonight - contains - the rather - important - role - of - a - young - girl - called - Sarah...
How could I not know that, Mum? I've been stuck with Ophelia and Aurora fighting over the stupid part for the last two days!
said very fast and with a lot of annoyance
Well it looks like the fight has proved too much for both of them then.

What?

Oh **Hyppolita** – do I have to spell it out?

YES! I have **no** idea what you're talking about!

Right then – Octavia crippled herself and has a nose like a purple balloon –

Yes, Mother, I was there when **Ophelia** –

And... the **other** one... has lost her voice.

Aurora? She can't have! Her voice is loud enough to fill an airport.

Not today, I gather... Today she can't even raise a squeak.

I suddenly remembered Nigel's warnings last night. I tried <u>not</u> to see the funny side... and failed.

So that's why I'm asking how well you know the play.
sudden failure to see funny side as realization begins to dawn.
How well I know the... Mum! Mum? Surely you're not - you can't be... NO WAY!
I'm sure you could do it, Pollypop! It's not such a big part... You're not totally stupid, and you must have picked up some shred of talent from me somewhere along the line.
She knows how to build a girl's confidence.
You must be joking!
said from deep inside duvet
Oh come on, Polly-Poodle - the show can't go on without you!
ABSOLUTELY NO WAY!

I can't say the dress rehearsal went well...

... So the afternoon was spent going over my scenes one by one with the ~~fellivant~~ relevant actors, who ~~valient~~ valiantly tried not to mention that they'd all had to cancel their massage bookings at the health club.

At 5 o'clock Nigel clapped his hands.

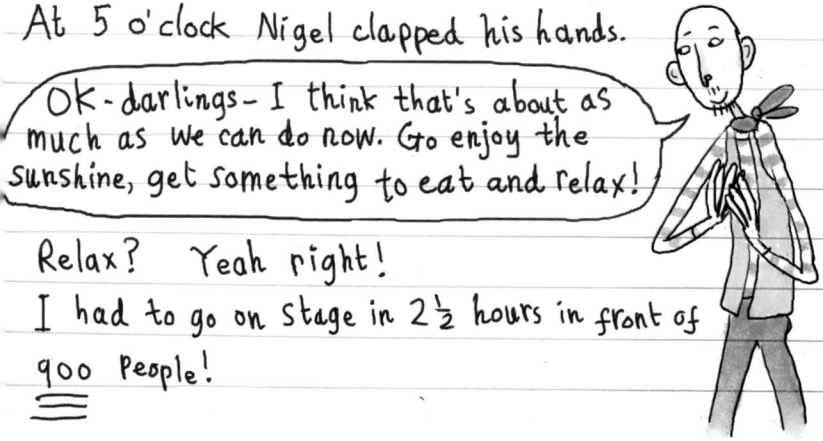

Relax? Yeah right!

I had to go on stage in 2½ hours in front of 900 people!

Could a nightmare get much worse?
Yes...
Polly - What a TOTAL DISASTER...
Me trying not to look like I'm going to cry.
That ... DRESS!!! It's DREADFUL! Way too BIG! But fear not! Janie from wardrobe will be here in just a mo- to wave her wand.
So I hadn't got the sack!
... Which meant I still had to go on tonight!
Oh and, Polly-
He was still here-

You're going to be great!
Exit Nigel, leaving me with my mouth hanging open– NOT A GOOD LOOK – which Will arrived just in time to witness.
Hey Poll, are you coming to get something to eat?
Hold on, you lovebirds! I've got to pin her up before you can disappear off into the sunset!
THANKS, Janie from Wardrobe! Better with pins than with people is my guess.

Things then went from bad to worse. Janie from wardrobe got me to climb onto a table, and stand there like a dummy - a very very red dummy - for about 100 years, while she pinned the dress.

FUN ???!!!

When I was due on stage in a couple of hours?

Fun was definitely not an option.
Had she said -

Go off and sit in front of a burger and try not to puke

- I could have done that.

In fact I did do that...
for approximately
one hour.

Then back to the theatre for...

Costume (feeling sick)...

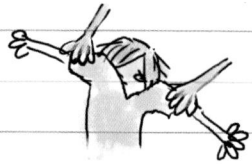

Make-up (feeling sicker)...

Wig (sicker still)...

And suddenly
there I was
in the wings,
peeping
out at this
MASSIVE
audience,
waiting for my
first cue...

AGGH!

MY ARTIST'S IMPRESSION

I can't say for sure if I said my lines at the right time we'd got to the very last scene.

OF THE PLAY

or in the right place, but in what felt like seconds

← me acting like mad!

And then it was all over, and I was being hauled on stage for the curtain call.

I'd got through it and... I'd quite enjoyed it! There were even a couple of moments when I almost believed I was Sarah and that I had a brother, and we were on the run!

But just when I thought it was finally over, they all started talking about getting ready for the party.

NO WAY was I going to that.

I've been to too many Opening Night parties – standing around in dark corners while actors go:

Daahling. you were Sensational!

Simply marvellous, Luvvy!

... to my mum.

So I sneaked back to the dressing room, got my jeans on and headed for the door.

Where do you think you're off to, Sweetie?

BUM. Nigel was blocking my exit, ~~brandesh~~ brandishing a huge carrier bag.

I sent Donna off this afternoon to pick you out something for the party - **just** in case it slipped your mind. So – see you there!

Orlando

And off he skipped - leaving me with a big bag, an open mouth and this

THE COLISEUM

PARKWAY DRIVE, SAN FRANCISCO

welcomes

Polly Price

to

Torn Asunder

Opening party

Friday 27th July

10 pm onwards

I looked in the bag. Inside was one of those shimmering dresses I'd fallen for in Orlando's. There was even a matching pair of satin ballet pumps in my size!

Janie from wardrobe helped to make me ~~unfekon~~ ~~unreckoni~~ unrecognizable and then took this picture → to prove it!

Before I could change my mind we were all whooshed off to The ~~Collesium~~ Coliseum, and into a sea of flashing cameras.

I just concentrated on getting through them all without tripping over, and I'd finally made it into the Banqueting Suite when Will nudged me and pointed.

Ophelia and Aurora were looking straight at us – without any obvious sign of affection.

To be honest I was a bit surprised to see them.

Before I could answer we were suddenly surrounded...

Hardly surprising I suppose - she is my child after all. One day she may even have the power to move an audience...
Did you coach her yourself?
Of course! I taught her **everything!** From the cradle she has been watching and learning - haven't you, Polly-Petal?

Amos, Sweetie - why don't you get that gorgeous photographer over here to do a picture of the two of us together? A mother and daughter feature! Now wouldn't that be something for your paper! Hyppolita, stand here—
Walter, dear - run along now and find something to eat - you look famished.
IRON SHOULDER GRIP
SHOVE

ABOUT AN HOUR LATER

I'm sitting in one of the toilets trying to avoid EVERYONE.

As soon as my mum released me I tried to find Will to say sorry. He was right on the other side of the room, sitting on a huge sofa with Felix, balancing plates of food on their laps. They totally looked like they didn't want to be ~~interupt~~ interrupted, so I just stayed where I was, remembering how much I hate Opening nights.

But a few seconds later, standing by yourself feeling lonely seemed like a really cosy option — because Ophelia and Aurora were heading straight for me... and something told me they weren't coming over to say...

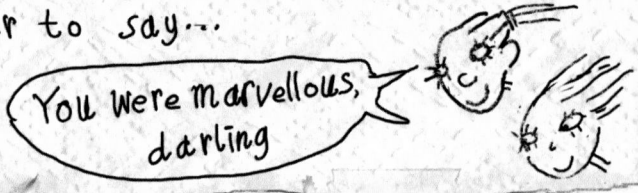

Fortunately crutches slow you down.
Even more fortunately ballet shoes don't.

I had already spotted the Ladies sign →

(an old and highly useful escape strategy)

so I ~~hertal~~ hurtled straight for it.

TROUBLE is I've now totally caught up with everything that's happened and I'm COMPLETELY

STARVING.

Ophelia and Aurora must have gone by now.

I suppose I have to leave here sometime.

Might as well be now.

ME

~~ignominiously~~ hiding in the toilets (very posh and shiny with lots of ~~marbet~~ marble everywhere - like a palace!)

(I stupidly left my diary in the Banqueting ~~swe~~ Suite)

This is much harder to write on.

MUCH LATER

I put my head down (this way you can't catch anyone's eye) and charged towards the food table.

A crutch was blocking my way.

How did mice, bats and horses get into this?

Aggh! I've run out of notebook - so I'm adding some paper I borrowed from Will.

loud enough to make the whole room go quiet
You've been planning it all along, haven't you? Hanging around us, sucking up to the boys, sneaking about, spying, secretly learning our lines ... until you finally got what you wanted. Only, I am afraid - Little Miss Thief - you can't steal TALENT! Or good press reviews! And I'm sure you won't need me to tell you you were a complete DISASTER on stage - everyone thought so.
me - trying to look like I'm not going to cry for the 2nd time tonight
Actually - I thought Polly's Performance was immensely moving...
Nigel was grinning down at me! Then suddenly people all around joined in...
I thought so too
She's a fine little actress!
Utterly believable

Then one of the reporters said:

Both the kids were great tonight. How about a shot of the girl and her brother?

And the next thing I knew, Will was being dragged over and they were taking pictures of us both!

I got given this one!

When they finally finished with us, Will turned to me...

You'd better come and rescue your plate of food, Poll. I saw Aurora eyeing up your sausage roll just now!

My plate of food?

We've been patiently waiting for the **CHILD-STAR** to come and grace us with her presence!

And as I squeezed on the sofa between Will and Felix, stuffing what was left of the sausage roll into my mouth, I suddenly knew that this had to be the end of the **BEST** day ever–

and **NOTHING** could mess that up...

... Absolutely **NOTHING!!!**

SAN FRANCISCO COURIER

THIS WEEK ON THE STAGE

Letitia Milton *reviews*

TORN ASUNDER

****

Rondo Theatre

This gruelling, yet touching World War Two drama is beautifully directed by Nigel Dillane, featuring an all-British cast fresh from London's West End.

Daniel Hopkins, as ever, is chillingly powerful in the role of Gestapo Officer Otto Schmidt. And American audiences are treated to the surprising casting of Arabella Diamonte in the role of Elsa, the mother whose life is torn asunder by the horrific events in Germany at the time. Diamonte plays the role with characteristic gusto, which at times seems just a little ebullient in the circumstances.

An unexpected bonus is the debut performance of Hyppolita Price, real-life daughter playing stage daughter, Sarah. She and William Granger (Hugo) were genuinely compelling as brother and sister on the run.

I'd also like to make a special mention of Ron Slimey as the dead officer, who lies remarkably still at the front of the stage for practically twenty minutes.

All in all a great night out!

Arabella Diamonte with her daughter, Hyppolita, last night at the opening of ***Torn Asunder.***

I looked this up. It means cheerful and full of energy or boiling and agitated!!!

I wasn't too sure about compelling – it means forcing attention – but ~~tHiff~~ everyone says it's a good thing!!

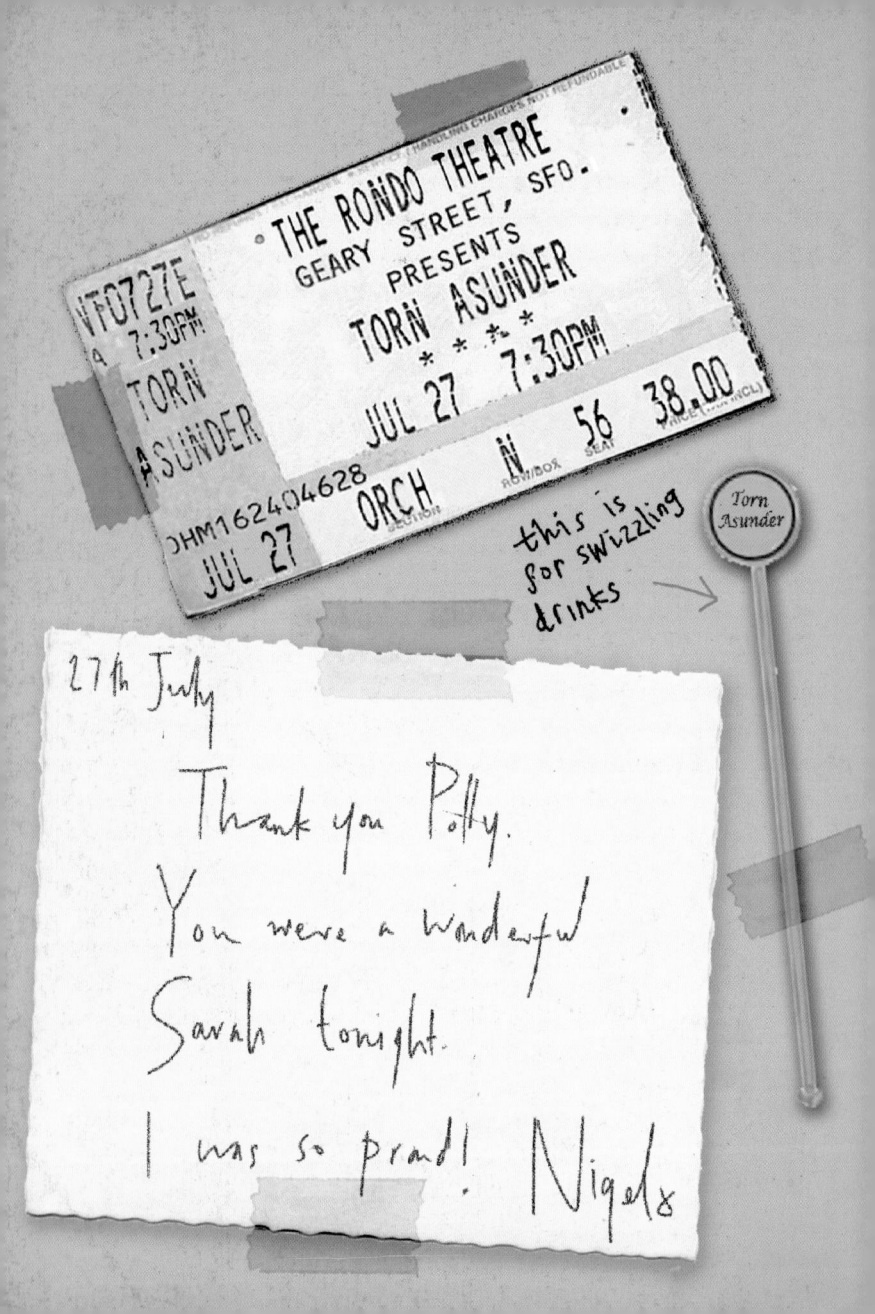
THE RONDO THEATRE
GEARY STREET, SFO.
PRESENTS
TORN ASUNDER
* * * *
JUL 27 7:30PM
ORCH N 56 38.00
NT0727E
7:30PM
TORN
ASUNDER
JUL 27
this is for swizzling drinks
Torn Asunder
27th July
Thank you Polly.
You were a wonderful
Sarah tonight.
I was so proud!
Nigel x

WILL
WILL
WILL
Dr William Granger
Will Granger (Hugo) played the title role in Oliver at the Dewkesbury Theatre; Prince Edward in Richard III at The Fleece, Stratford; and Charlie, in the Hillfield Players production of Every Little Helps. Will enjoys playing football and listening to music. He is studying for his GCSEs next summer, and hopes to become a doctor.
W.G
THE COLISEUM
welcomes
Torn Asunder
Friday 27th July
genuine coaster from party (with Ron's wine stain)
rose - from Mum's Opening Night flowers

Ron Slimey (Officer Blythe)
Slimey trained at The Drama Institute. TV credits include: ***The Bill, Crown Street***, and ***Ambulance Emergency.*** Film credits include: ***Zombies 111, Captain Goo, Pirate Babies*** and ***Lime Green Beetlejuice.***

I've watched Zombies III 4 times and still haven't spotted Ron.

Daniel Hopkins (Otto Schmidt)
is probably best known as TV detective Inspector Dysmal. Other TV roles include Melmoth in the cult witch series ***Sisters***, and Jaz in ***Dad's Disasters***. His film credits include: ***City Woman, Sad and Sadder. The Moonlight Saga.*** and ***Vampires Suck.*** Theatre appearances include Sebastian in ***Twelfth Night*** with The Contemporary Shakespeare Company, and ***The Harridan Wife*** at The Apollo theatre, London.

I LOVE the Moonlight Saga. I've seen it 9 times!

Arabella Diamonte (Elsa) played Cruella Deville, in the Surbiton Playhouse award winning panto; ***Snow White and the 101 Dalmations***. She co-starred with Daniel Hopkins in ***The Harridan Wife*** at London's Apollo Theatre, and played the title role in ***The Witch of North Shields***, at The Dunstable Playhouse. Her TV credits include: Medusa, in ***The Monsters of Greek Legend*** for the BBC, and Demon Space Invader, in the popular C5 series, ***Sisters***.

Need I say more

rogramme Notes (with important additions by Polly Price)

Aurora Stumps (Sarah) played Veruca Salt in the Hampstead Young Players production of ***Charlie and the Chocolate Factory,*** the title role in ***Princess Smartie-Pants*** at the Griffin Theatre in Ipswich, and Lavinia Frost in ***Mean Girls*** at the Chelsea Apollo. She plans to be a musical actress when she leaves school.

Wonder how Aurora managed to get that part?

Nigel Dillane - *Director*
Dillane began his career in the theatre as an actor, but made his directing debut in the Daggenham Globe production of ***The Fat Lady Sings.*** After assisting Sir Bevan Bunn on several award-winning productions, he became associate director with Rhapsody Theatre. His West End credits include: ***Lock up your Sons*** and ***'Tis Pity She's a Bore.***

It was definitely a pity Mum made me go and watch this but I suppose the clue was in the title.

Ophelia Bristle (Sarah) played Harriet Hyacinth-Smythe in the popular TV series ***Poshford Abbey,*** and Melissa Mandrake in ***The Poisonous Friend.*** Films include ***After the Werewolf*** and ***Pride and Presents.*** Ophelia intends to be a World Leader when she grows up.

!!!

Dear Ophelia.. so humble in her ambition.

LIBRARIES

Whatever happens please please please...
Polly Price's
Totally
TAKE 45
SECRET Diary
Reality TV Nightmare
me, POLLY PRICE (helpless victim)
Sue Shulman

...DON'T read my other tragick diaries!
COMING SOON!
Polly Price's
Totally
SECRET Diary
Mum in Love
Yuck!
AVAILABLE FROM
RANDOM HOUSE
CHILDREN'S BOOKS
www.kidsatrandom.co.uk
www.pollyprice.co.uk

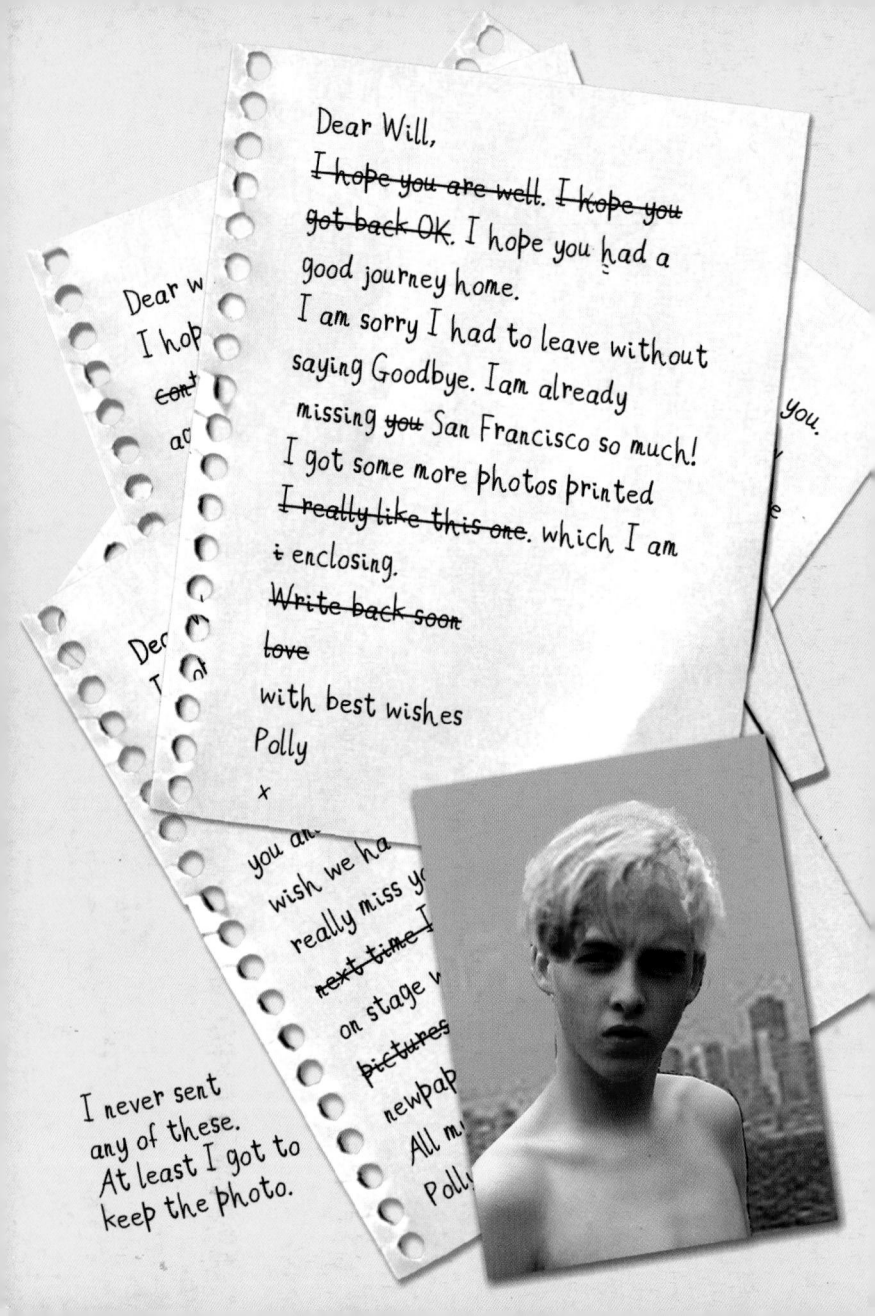
Dear Will,
~~I hope you are well~~. ~~I hope you got back OK~~. I hope you had a good journey home.
I am sorry I had to leave without saying Goodbye. Iam already missing ~~you~~ San Francisco so much!
I got some more photos printed ~~I really like this one~~. which I am ~~i~~ enclosing.
~~Write back soon~~
~~love~~
with best wishes
Polly
x
I never sent any of these. At least I got to keep the photo.